Sam
and the
Bag

Sam
and the
Bag

Alison Jeffries

Illustrated by Dan Andreasen

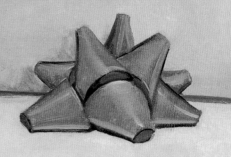

Green Light Readers
Harcourt, Inc.
Orlando Austin New York San Diego London

Max ran into the bag.

Hap ran into the bag.

Sam ran up the bag.

Sam ran down the bag.

Can Sam jump in?

Yes, Sam can jump in!

Oh, Sam!

FOLLOW THE ANIMALS

Sam the cat can run and jump.
Can you move like an animal?
Play animal follow-the-leader with your friends and find out!

1. Choose an animal.

2. Say the animal follow-the-leader rhyme on the next page.

3. Move like the animal.

4. Pick a new leader—and a new animal—and play again!

A little **duck** went out to play.
 Back and forth it moved this way.
Come along and follow me,
 A little **duck** is what you'll be!

Think About It

1. What do Max and Hap do at the beginning of the story?

2. What does Sam do when Max and Hap are in the bag?

3. What happens when Sam jumps into the bag?

4. Do you think Max and Hap will let Sam play with them again? Why or why not?

5. What do you think Sam learns?

Acting Like Sam

Make a finger puppet of Sam.
Use it to act out the story. Take it
off when Sam jumps into the bag.

When I'm Bigger

Soon Sam will be bigger, like his friends
Max and Hap. What will you be like when
you are bigger? Draw a picture and write
a sentence about being bigger. Then share
your picture and sentence with a friend!

Meet the Illustrator

For *Sam and the Bag*, Dan Andreasen drew sketches of the pictures first. Once he was happy with them, he covered the background with a color called burnt sienna to give it a special glow. Then he used oil paints to make Sam and his friends.

When Dan Andreasen's daughter was in kindergarten, her teacher asked, "What does your Daddy do?" His daughter said, "He colors!"

For information about permission to reproduce selections from this book,
please write Permissions, Houghton Mifflin Harcourt Publishing Company
215 park Avenue South NY NY 10003.

www.hmhbooks.com

First Green Light Readers edition 2004
Green Light Readers is a trademark of Harcourt, Inc., registered in the
United States of America and/or other jurisdictions.

Library of Congress Cataloging-in-Publication Data
Jeffries, Alison (Alison A.)
Sam and the bag/Alison Jeffries; illustrated by Dan Andreasen.
p. cm.
"Green Light Readers."
Summary: Sam the cat joins his friends Hap and Max in playing with a bag.
[1. Cats—Fiction.] I. Andreasen, Dan, ill. II. Title. III. Series: Green Light Reader.
PZ7.J3665Sam 2004
[E]—dc22 2003018905
ISBN 978-0-15-205152-5
ISBN 978-0-15-205151-8 pb

SCP 10 9 8
4500377330

Ages 4-6
Grade: K-I
Guided Reading Level: C
Reading Recovery Level: 4

Green Light Readers
For the reader who's ready to GO!

"A must-have for any family with a beginning reader."—*Boston Sunday Herald*

"You can't go wrong with adding several copies of these terrific books to your beginning-to-read collection."—*School Library Journal*

"A winner for the beginner."—*Booklist*

Five Tips to Help Your Child Become a Great Reader

1. Get involved. Reading aloud to and with your child is just as important as encouraging your child to read independently.

2. Be curious. Ask questions about what your child is reading.

3. Make reading fun. Allow your child to pick books on subjects that interest her or him.

4. Words are everywhere—not just in books. Practice reading signs, packages, and cereal boxes with your child.

5. Set a good example. Make sure your child sees YOU reading.

Why Green Light Readers Is the Best Series for Your New Reader

• Created exclusively for beginning readers by some of the biggest and brightest names in children's books

• Reinforces the reading skills your child is learning in school

• Encourages children to read—and finish—books by themselves

• Offers extra enrichment through fun, age-appropriate activities unique to each story

• Incorporates characteristics of the Reading Recovery program used by educators

• Developed with Harcourt School Publishers and credentialed educational consultants